# Twenty Years On

A little hare in a field tells a big hare how much he loves him using simple body language and some elementary geography. *Guess How Much I Love You* is a light-hearted story for a big one and a wee one to share; you turn the pages, you read the words, you do the actions and you play the game. This evening, somewhere in the world, a mum or dad will be reading Guess with someone special. I'd like to share with you one comment a father sent me. He wrote: "On good nights my little girl loves me all the way to the moon, but on bad nights she only loves me to the door." If you're a parent (or a grandparent like myself), here's hoping that you mostly make it to the moon.

And back...

*Sam McBratney*

Two little hares hopped out of my pen
onto the paper, into the meadow, and then far away.

Pictures, like children, can have unexpected
and unimagined lives all of their own,
as they find their way in the wide, wide world.

*Anita Jeram*

# GUESS
## HOW MUCH
### I LOVE YOU

To Lydia, Ella, Adam,
Jack, Daniel and Sam,
S.MᶜB.

To Liz with love,
A.J.

First published 1994 by Walker Books Ltd
87 Vauxhall Walk, London SE11 5HJ

This edition published 2015

10 9 8 7 6 5 4 3 2

Text © 1994 Sam MᶜBratney
Illustrations © 1994 Anita Jeram

Guess How Much I Love You™ is a trademark
of Walker Books Ltd, London.

The right of Sam MᶜBratney and Anita Jeram to be identified as
author and illustrator respectively of this work has been asserted by
them in accordance with the Copyright, Designs and Patents Act 1988.

This book has been typeset in Cochin.

Printed in Malaysia

British Library Cataloguing in Publication Data:
a catalogue record for this book is available from the British Library.

ISBN 978-1-4063-6235-0

www.walker.co.uk

# GUESS HOW MUCH I LOVE YOU

Written by

## Sam M<sup>c</sup>Bratney

Illustrated by

## Anita Jeram

WALKER BOOKS

AND SUBSIDIARIES

LONDON · BOSTON · SYDNEY · AUCKLAND

Little Nutbrown Hare, who was going to bed, held on tight to Big Nutbrown Hare's very long ears.

He wanted to be sure that Big
Nutbrown Hare was listening.
"Guess how much
I love you," he said.

"Oh, I don't think I could guess that,"
said Big Nutbrown Hare.

"This much," said Little
Nutbrown Hare, stretching out
his arms as wide as they could go.

Big Nutbrown Hare had even longer arms. "But I love YOU this much," he said.

Hmm, that is a lot, thought Little Nutbrown Hare.

"I love you as high as I can reach," said Little Nutbrown Hare.

"I love you as high as *I* can reach," said Big Nutbrown Hare.

That is quite high, thought Little Nutbrown Hare. I wish I had arms like that.

Then Little
Nutbrown Hare
had a good idea.
He tumbled
upside down
and reached
up the tree
trunk with
his feet.

"I love you
all the way up
to my toes!"
he said.

"And *I* love you
all the way up
to your toes," said
Big Nutbrown Hare,
swinging him up
over his head.

"I love you
as high as
I can HOP!"
laughed Little
Nutbrown Hare,

bouncing up

and down.

"But I love you as high as
*I* can hop," smiled Big
Nutbrown Hare – and he
hopped so high that his ears
touched the branches above.

That's good
hopping,
thought
Little
Nutbrown
Hare.
I wish I
could hop
like that.

"I love you all the way down the lane as far as the river," cried Little Nutbrown Hare.

"I love you across the river
and over the hills," said
Big Nutbrown Hare.

That's very far, thought
Little Nutbrown Hare.
He was almost too sleepy
to think any more.

Then he looked beyond the
thorn bushes, out into the big
dark night. Nothing could
be further than the sky.

"I love you right up to
the MOON," he said,
and closed his eyes.

"Oh, that's far," said
Big Nutbrown Hare.
"That is very,
very far."

Big Nutbrown Hare settled
Little Nutbrown Hare
into his bed of leaves.

He leaned over
and kissed him
good night.

Then he lay down close by
and whispered with a smile,
"I love you right up to the moon –

AND BACK."